Puffin Books

DRAGONRISE

'If only I knew what Dragonrise was,' said Tom in despair. 'If I don't know what it is, I'm sure to miss it.'

'Nonsense,' said the dragon, just behind his ear. 'It's Dragonrise now. That's why I'm here.'

And there he was: a small, smart, green and gold, friendly-looking dragon, sitting on Tom's eiderdown, just as he had done the night before.

Tom was fascinated by the dragon, who seemed to have had a truly adventurous past fighting ravening octocats, travelling underground to the West, breathing fire, and devouring hapless maidens whenever he could find them. Tom was a little bothered by the bit about devouring maidens and he began to worry that his new friend might be getting hungry – hapless maidens being in short supply these days. He did his best by offering all sorts of tasty morsels as a substitute but the dragon didn't seem to be all that interested. Then Tom's elder sister, Sarah, did something that he could not forgive – and he realized that the dragon could help him take a very unusual revenge!

Being friends with a dragon – and keeping him secret – is far from easy and Tom ends up in some hair-raising situations, which will have young readers chuckling with delight as they read from page to page. For six- to nine-year-olds.

Illustrated by Liz Graham-Yooll

D1149232

Kathryn Cave

Dragonrise

Illustrated by Liz Graham-Yooll

Puffin Books

Puffin Books, Penguin Books Ltd, Harmondsworth, Middlesex, England
Viking Penguin Inc., 40 West 23rd Street, New York, New York 10010, U.S.A.
Penguin Books Australia Ltd, Ringwood, Victoria, Australia
Penguin Books Canada Limited, 2801 John Street, Markham, Ontario, Canada L3R 1B4
Penguin Books (N.Z.) Ltd, 182–190 Wairau Road, Auckland 10, New Zealand

First published 1984
Reprinted 1984, 1985, 1986 (twice)

Made and printed in Great Britain by
Richard Clay Ltd, Bungay, Suffolk
Filmset in 12/14pt Monophoto Times

For Eleanor and Joseph

Chapter One

In a small, not quite dark bedroom next to the bathroom at number 27 Wellington Gardens, lay a seven-year-old boy called Tom, not quite asleep. He was twirling a finger in his hair and singing to himself in a dreamy way as follows:

> 'Paddington, Paddington, Paddington Pie,
> A fly can't fish and a fish can't fly.
> Ask me a question and I'll reply
> "Paddington, Paddington, Paddington Pie."'

When he was halfway through singing this for the nineteenth time, something quite unexpected happened.

'Ask me a question,' Tom chanted softly, 'and I'll reply ...'

'What's your name?' said an interested voice. It seemed to come from beneath the bed.

'Who's that?' All of a sudden Tom was wide awake and sitting bolt upright on his pillow. 'And what are you doing under my bed?'

'Ah,' said the voice. 'I thought you wouldn't *really* say "Paddington, Paddington, Paddington Pie." It would hardly have been worth taking the trouble to say hello if that was all you could manage in the way of conversation. Now we've got that cleared up I'll be happy to come out and introduce myself.'

While Tom sat frozen on top of his pillow there came a scuffling and scraping from underneath his bed. The first thing to appear was a green, spiky tail, broad and pointed like the tail of a kangaroo. This was closely followed by a pair of stout green legs. Each leg had a foot with bright red claws. A scaly back, green with gold zigzag markings, had some trouble working clear of the bedsprings and Tom heard the voice say 'Bother' crossly before, with a final wriggle, the creature's front legs and head were freed and Tom found himself face to face with a small, smart, green and gold, friendly-looking dragon.

'I expect,' said the creature amiably, 'you're at a loss for words. Strictly speaking it should be you, as a human being and my host, who makes the introductions, but I'm not one to stand on ceremony. I'm Dragon. How do you do?' So saying he held out his paw.

Tom took a deep breath (it seemed to be the first

he'd taken for several minutes) and put out his hand. The paw, he noticed, had seven claws on it, neatly shaped into points and suspiciously sharp looking.

'I'm Tom Smith,' he said. 'I'm very pleased to meet you and I'm sorry if I seemed rude. It was just that I didn't know there were dragons nowadays so it came as a surprise to find you under my bed.'

'Think nothing of it.' The dragon's handshake was a hearty squeeze that made Tom pull his hand back in a hurry and suck his right fore-finger, which had come too close for comfort to one of the red claws.

'Is that a wound?' asked the dragon, with concern.

'Your claws are a bit sharp, that's all. It's nothing really.' Tom spoke apologetically. He didn't like to offend anyone, least of all a dragon. For the same reason he let the dragon lift his hand up for closer inspection in the moonlight that was filtering through the bedroom curtains. The dragon examined the scratched finger with a tinge of disapproval.

'Your scales are thin,' he said, and shook his head, sending a gentle puff of warm air from his nostrils onto Tom's wrist. 'Still, the scales often harden as you get older so we won't give up hope yet. You could try eating carrots,' he added thoughtfully.

'People aren't supposed to have scales like you.' Tom wondered how he was going to get his hand back to safety. The dragon had turned it over now and was studying the other side.

'I've never seen such a weak collection of claws in all my born days,' he said, more disapproving than before. 'You'll never catch anything if you cut the ends straight across like that. How are you going to rip or slash or shred with claws like these, I'd like to know?'

Meeting the dragon's severe gaze, Tom was about to answer that ripping, slashing and shredding were not in general encouraged at number 27 Wellington Gardens, or at his school, but the dragon swept on before he could put the thought into words. 'It's a good thing for you that I came along when I did, that's plain to see.'

Tom had indeed been wondering just how and why the dragon had turned up as he had, but this was the first chance he had had to ask any questions. Before the dragon could open his mouth again – Tom felt sure he was going to go back to the topic of scales, claws and carrots at any moment – Tom beat him to it.

'How did you get under my bed?' he began. 'Where do you come from how long have you been here what do you eat and why aren't you in my encyclopedia?'

Instead of being put out by getting so many questions at once the dragon looked highly pleased. 'Interest in dragons is the beginning of all wisdom,' he commented with approval. 'What do you want to know first?'

'How did you get here?'

The dragon looked mildly surprised. 'The usual way.'

'Through the front door and up the stairs?' asked Tom, round-eyed. How could he have done it without being seen? No one moved a step inside the house without his sister Sarah poking her head up to see what was happening.

But that was not what the dragon had meant. He laughed pleasantly. 'The usual way for a *dragon*,' he said.

That was as far as Tom could get. What was the usual way for a dragon? Oh, normal procedure. And what was normal procedure? Just routine.

Tom switched his line of attack. 'Well, tell me where you come from, then, and that sort of thing.'

This was the kind of invitation you don't have to give a dragon twice. The dragon settled himself down on the carpet like someone with a long story to tell. Tom snuggled deeper under the bedclothes and watched the dragon's green scales glimmer in the pale moonlight.

'I was hatched in the year 1143 (counting from the Conquest of Wales by the dragons of Outer Cornwall). My family were poor but ancient and I passed the first five hundred years of my life in the magnificent forest of –' he said a name that sounded something like Hebden ap Cwumbeer.

'Where?' asked Tom.

'Just off the Andover bypass. And there I lived, as happy as the nights were long. But then, when I was scarcely five hundred and one –' here the dragon lowered his voice to a whisper, and Tom's eyes widened.

At this point, however, the second interruption of the night took place. It was less surprising than the dragon's appearance and much less welcome. Tom's sister, Sarah, slept just along the passage, and her door made a noise every time she went in or out of her room. Just now it gave the most tremendous creak.

'What's that?' asked the dragon, rising on all fours. His spikes were sticking up on end, to Tom's delight, like the fur of an angry cat.

'It's Sarah. My sister,' he whispered. 'I won't let her

in, though.' He jumped out of bed and planted his shoulder against the door, just in time. Sarah's voice came from the other side, sounding cross.

'If you don't stop making all that noise I'll tell Mummy. I can't read when there's so much bouncing and muttering going on. Let me in.'

'Go away,' said Tom, red in the face. It's no easy matter to keep a door shut when the person pushing on the other side is almost two years older than you and a lot bigger. He looked back over his shoulder at the dragon for help, but all he could see was a green tail twitching out from under the bed. He tried to think of a clever way to get rid of Sarah, but as usual without success. 'Go away or I'll ... I'll bite you,' he hissed in desperation.

There was a pause while Sarah, on the other side of the door, tried to decide whether or not Tom was serious.

On the one hand he had never bitten her, or anyone else so far as she knew, in his whole life. On the other hand, there was always the first time – and she might even catch something nasty.

She stopped pushing on the door. 'Well, don't forget it: if you let out one more squeak I'll complain to Mummy and you'll get told off for being awake.'

Sarah's footsteps thumped off down the corridor, her door creaked and then there was silence. Tom took his shoulder away from the door cautiously and tiptoed back to the bed. By squatting down he could see the dragon's green eyes shining in the gloom underneath, and the glow of the warm air that came puffing from its nose.

'She's gone,' he whispered. 'Please go on and tell me what happened when you were five hundred and one.'

'It's too dangerous now,' said the dragon with regret, and nothing Tom said could persuade him to change his mind.

'But when will I see you again?' said Tom at last.

'Tomorrow. At Dragonrise.'

'Dragonrise? What's that? And when does it happen?'

'Go back to bed and I'll tell you.'

With one last, loving look at the dragon, Tom climbed reluctantly back onto his bed. The dragon's voice came floating up to him through the mattress.

> 'When sunlight fades and starlight flies
> Look west to Wales
> For Dragonrise.
> Then tired day sheds its disguise,
> The night brings truth,
> And Dragonrise
> Makes bright the skies.'

'But *when* tomorrow shall I look for you?' asked Tom urgently when the dragon seemed to have stopped. 'And what *is* Dragonrise?'

The dragon sighed. 'All right, if you insist I'll work it out. Today's April the 13th, and thirteen take away seven is five –'

'No it's not, it's six.'

'Add four and you have nine –'

'Ten,' Tom pleaded, without the dragon paying the slightest attention.

'– and take away the number you first thought of,

adjust for summertime and there we are. Dragonrise will be at exactly 8.05 tomorrow evening. Don't,' he went on, with severity, 'don't ask me if I'm sure because I am and even if I wasn't I jolly well wouldn't go through all that rigmarole again. Now shut your eyes and go to sleep, or you'll be too tired to have any fun tomorrow night.'

Tom shut his eyes, then opened them again. 'You still haven't told me what Dragonrise *is*,' he pointed out.

'You'll see,' was the dragon's answer. 'You'll see.'

Chapter Two

Everyone knows that the two longest days in the year are the day before your birthday and the day before Christmas. Even so, Tom couldn't help feeling that the day after he met the dragon was longer still.

He was up, dressed and eating his cornflakes before Sarah had so much as opened her eyes.

He was sitting in the car ready for the trip to school before Sarah had cleaned her teeth. In fact he was so early that his mother spent some time searching round the house for him before she finally caught sight of him waiting in the back of the car.

But no matter how Tom tried to make the day pass quickly, the clock went on ticking at its normal speed and not a second faster.

At school Tom raced through all his work. Mrs Steel, his teacher, was not pleased. 'Messy work,' she wrote on Tom's colouring of a space ship, which Tom thought was hardly polite.

'What terrible writing,' was her comment when she saw what Tom had written describing Peter and Jane's visit to the seashore. Tom had to do a whole page of b's and d's as extra writing practice.

Even playtime was not a success. When Tom tried to take his mind off the dragon by wrestling John

Murphy, who was big and fun, he got pushed over. Then Sarah came to tell John Murphy off and she got pushed over too.

'It's all your fault,' she told Tom as she limped off to the medical room to have her knee cleaned up.

'I didn't do anything,' he shouted after her. John Murphy wouldn't play wrestling any more so the rest of playtime was miserable.

Tom was so eager to get to bed that night that his mother began to wonder if he was sickening for something. 'It's only six o'clock,' she said. 'Let me have a look at your tongue.'

Tom showed her his tongue and let her feel his forehead, and was allowed to have his own way. He had his curtains drawn and his lights out by six-thirty, which was a record. He wanted to be absolutely ready for Dragonrise, whenever that should happen to arrive. Since the dragon's arithmetic was so special, Tom felt that the magic hour might turn out to be well before 8.05.

Seven o'clock struck, however, and there was no dragon. Seven-thirty. Tom looked under the bed for the fifteenth time and tried to remember the dragon's precise words on the subject of Dragonrise.

At eight o'clock he remembered and, kneeling up on the bed, flung his bedroom curtains wide.

'Look west to Wales.' Which way was west? He couldn't remember. The sky looked dark in every direction.

'If only I knew what Dragonrise was,' said Tom in despair. 'If I don't know what it is, I'm sure to miss it.'

'Nonsense,' said the dragon just behind his ear. 'It's Dragonrise now. That's why I'm here.'

And there he was, not under the bed this time but sitting comfortably on top of Tom's eiderdown as if he'd never been anywhere else.

For a moment Tom was too delighted to speak. 'Oh Dragon, I thought you'd never come,' he said at last. 'The sky was so dark and cloudy out there. I thought it was supposed to get bright at Dragonrise. Why didn't it?'

For just a second it seemed to Tom that the dragon looked less cheerful than before. 'That verse about Dragonrise was written long ago, Tom. There were more dragons about then than there are mice today.

At Dragonrise – which I suppose you would call night-fall – we would all look up at the black sky and salute the coming of the dark. Like this,' he added, his eyes lighting suddenly. 'Open the window.'

This was something Tom was strictly forbidden to do, in case he fell out, but he obeyed the dragon instantly. It was lucky that he pulled back the curtains too because the dragon immediately opened his mouth and sent a tongue of flame licking past Tom's hand and shooting out into the darkness. A second, no more, and then it was gone, and the dragon was just sitting beside Tom the same as before – only, perhaps, looking a little more pleased with himself than previously.

'I'm glad to see I haven't lost the knack. Well, when hundreds and thousands and millions –'

'– and trillions,' suggested Tom.

'Trillions indeed,' the dragon acknowledged gravely. 'When all those dragons, too many to be counted, all over the face of the earth did that at the same time, it certainly did make bright the skies, just as the poem said. It's forbidden nowadays, of course, but,' and the dragon lowered his voice, 'we all do it now and then.'

'Why is it forbidden?'

The dragon looked startled. 'Don't be silly. Suppose we started celebrating Dragonrise in a town like this. Even out in the country it would be almost as bad. There'd be people ringing up fire brigades, calling the police, telephoning newspapers. No end of fuss. We'd be lucky not to end up in the reptile house at the zoo or as a stuffed exhibit in a natural history museum. Liberty is too precious to be thrown away like that. So no flame-throwing except in emergencies.'

'It does seem a shame,' said Tom wistfully. 'Couldn't you do it just once more?'

The dragon shook his head. 'The last dragon I know who broke the rule and got caught by the Dragonwatch was punished severely. What they did to him was almost too terrible to repeat. Shall I tell you what it was?'

Tom nodded, wordless.

The dragon lowered his voice to a whisper. 'They sent him to Wales.' He paused expectantly.

'How dreadful.' Tom could see he was meant to say something.

'There's worse to come. He had to stay there for fifty years.'

'That's *awful*,' said Tom, since something more seemed to be expected of him. Speaking just for himself, he rather liked Wales. The dragon, however, plainly felt differently.

'Of course the poor fellow was never the same again. He dried out eventually, after a couple of centuries or so, but the experience left a terrible mark on him. And with his example as a ghastly warning, the rest of us dragons take care before we break the rules.'

Tom had a lot of questions about the Dragonwatch, but the dragon's answers were confusing. They seemed to be some kind of dragon police force with almost limitless powers. It was plain that the dragon preferred not to discuss them. This was fine with Tom, so he was happy when the dragon suggested they take up the story of his life, beginning where they had left off the night before.

'Up until a dragon's five-hundred-and-first birthday – that was where I'd got up to, wasn't it? – he is of very little importance in dragon affairs. He must keep within strict boundaries, day and night, give way to senior dragons on paths, bridges and waterways, and keep flame-throwing down to a circle of not more than ten feet across. All the normal age restrictions, in fact. But at five hundred and one, all this comes to an end and there is a great battle of celebration with fire and feasting and fighting from dusk to dawn. Now, on my five-hundred-and-first birthday, which I remember as if it were only yesterday, dragons came from far and wide to join in the festivities. At Dragonrise the whole sky turned crimson, and then, as the glow faded, the

feasting began. As soon as that was under way, the fighting broke out.' The dragon paused with his eyes shut for a moment, as if picturing the scene.

'Was it very awful?' Tom wanted to know.

'Awful?' the dragon snorted. 'It was stupendous. Magnificent. Indescribable. It was the most wonderful day of battle in the whole dragon calendar. There was ripping and slashing and tearing and shredding. Scales flew through the air like meteors. The ground ran green with dragon's blood until we were up to our ankles. There were bodies everywhere. You've never seen a birthday party like it.'

Tom wasn't entirely sorry about that.

'And the ending was the most remarkable part of all. At one second I was wrestling with one of my young companions, a gold dragon from the Berkshire Downs, and the next I was surrounded by a sea of flame. The heat of the battle had set the whole forest ablaze. The trees flared up like torches. I felt the grass singe the tender part of my feet, in between the claws, and I heard my friend's voice cry, "Run, run for your life." So I ran. I ran as I never had before, until I had left the forest far behind and the flicker of the flames was no more than a faint glow in the sky behind me. When even that had vanished, still I ran. Not for fear, but for fun, to feel the night air rushing past me and the ground leaping under my feet. When dawn broke and I finally stopped, I found myself in Cornwall.'

'Do you mean you ran all the way to Cornwall in one night?' demanded Tom.

The dragon nodded.

'When we drive down to Cornwall in the car it takes us all day. You must be a very good runner.'

'I am,' said the dragon simply.

'We have to stop for a picnic on the way. Last year I had cucumber sandwiches and an apple.'

'I wouldn't have said no to a cucumber sandwich or two on the journey myself,' the dragon admitted. 'In fact I wouldn't even have said no to a carrot, a food of which I have never been fond. But I had to take what I could get – a few mouthfuls of grass for vitamins, and a bit of sand from the beach for filling. I was soon myself again.'

Tom felt glad that in no circumstances was he called upon to breakfast on grass and sand. On some things his own views and the dragon's were obviously miles apart.

'What do you like eating?' One of the nicest things about the dragon was the way he welcomed questions, so you needn't worry about asking too many.

'Can't you guess?'

Tom thought for a few seconds. 'Fish and chips?'

'No.'

'Sausages?'

'No.'

'Baked beans? Chocolate? Oranges? Nuts and raisins?'

The dragon went on shaking his head.

'I give up,' said Tom in despair.

'Think,' urged his friend. 'Think about the stories you've heard about us.'

Tom thought hard about dragon stories. There was

St George and the dragon, of course, but it wouldn't be good manners to mention that. It didn't seem to be what the dragon was getting at anyway.

'Go on, *think*. What was it that those interfering knights used to go round trying to rescue from dragons long ago?'

'Maidens?' guessed Tom.

'At last. Maidens, damsels, females. In a word, girls.' The dragon waited for Tom to express his approval.

Tom couldn't believe his ears. 'You mean you eat girls?'

'What else? When I can get them, that is. The supply isn't as reliable as it might be.'

It was at this point that Sarah's door opened. They could hear it creak, followed by the pit-pat of her bare feet along the hall. Tom had just time enough to notice that the dragon's spikes were standing on end and that he had a definitely hungry look about him before Tom found himself with his shoulder up against the bedroom door for the second night running.

The steps turned in at the bathroom. Tom heard the squeak of bare feet on the lino, the sound of water running, the clink of a glass. The steps squeaked and pattered away again. Sarah's door shut.

When Tom took his shoulder away from the door, he wasn't sure if he had been trying to keep Sarah out or the dragon in. It was rather a worrying thought.

The dragon had disappeared under the bed again, as he had the night before. Tom asked if he was coming out.

'Too many people about. We'll have to leave it until

tomorrow.' The dragon twanged a bedspring in a moody way, which Tom couldn't help feeling was somehow related to Sarah.

'Will Dragonrise be at the same time tomorrow?' he asked, to change the subject. The dragon immediately sounded happier.

'8.05 on the dot, or I'm a Welshman. Which heaven forbid,' he added, crossing his claws. 'Into bed, and I'll let you hear another of the dragon poems.'

As Tom lay with the eiderdown tucked up under his chin, he could hear the dragon chanting:

> 'Nightfall brings the magic hour
> When the dragons show their power.
> Dragonrise. Dragonrise.
> Dark and cloud our flames devour,
> Fierce as fire, bright as flower.
> Hide your eyes. Hide your eyes.
>
> Feel the wind of our desire
> Fan the flames and feed the fire.
> Fill the skies. Fill the skies.
> Sear the valleys, singe the mountains
> Till the flames shoot up like fountains.
> Dragonrise. Dragonrise.'

When the dragon's voice stopped, Tom thought the poem had ended. But later on, as he lay drowsing, he seemed to hear another rhyme.

> 'I don't eat sausages or cake,
> I don't like chips or apple bake,
> I don't want pie with cream in whirls –
> What dragons like to eat is girls.

>All in all, what could be fairer
>Than that I dine on sister . . .'

What came after that, Tom never knew; by that time he was sound asleep.

Chapter Three

At school the next day, Mrs Steel told the class to get out their colouring pencils. Tom was pleased. Drawing and colouring were better than almost anything else at school. The only thing he liked more was playing with John Murphy, and he couldn't do that during class.

'Today I want you to draw something that makes you feel happy,' said Mrs Steel. 'Can you think of something that makes you feel that way? What about you, Emma?'

Emma always had an answer for everything. She thought for a little and then said, 'Going to the swimming pool.'

'The seaside,' shouted Benjamin.

'A ride on the train.'

'Ice-cream.'

'Chocolate cake.'

'Riding a pony.'

'Toy shops.'

'Snowy mornings.'

Soon everyone was drawing. Mrs Steel came round to see how they were getting on. When she came to Tom, she stopped.

'What makes you feel happy, Tom?' He had his arm

round the sheet of paper so that she could only see a bit of the top corner.

'Dragonrise,' said Tom, carefully adding some red and yellow zigzags.

'Dragonflies?' said Mrs Steel. 'What an interesting idea. That's lovely, Tom.' Then she moved on to Sharon, who sat next to him. 'Mmm,' she said, in a different voice. 'Do you really like *purple* ice-cream, Sharon?'

Tom was given a gold star, the very best colour, for his drawing. Mrs Steel wrote 'Dragonflies' neatly on it at the top, and told Tom to take it to show Miss Andrews, the headmistress.

It didn't look much like any dragonflies she had ever seen, thought Miss Andrews. On the other hand, Mrs

Steel had been quite right to give the child a star for originality. She said all the proper things and Tom went back to his classroom feeling very pleased.

After school he showed his star to Sarah.

'I've had seven gold stars already this term,' she pointed out. 'Let me see your drawing again.'

Tom gave it to her.

'Where are the dragonflies?' she asked.

'There aren't any, silly,' said Tom calmly. 'And you've got it the wrong way up.'

'Oh.' Sarah turned the paper round and studied it. She tried shutting one eye; she tried shutting the other. Then she gave up. Tom took the drawing up to his bedroom and pinned it up on the corkboard above his bed.

Later that night, when their mother came in to say goodnight, Sarah said, 'Tom got a gold star today.'

'Yes.' Her mother tucked the sheets in round her. 'He did a lovely picture. Didn't he show it to you?'

'It was supposed to be a drawing of dragonflies,' Sarah went on in a puzzled voice. 'But when I asked where they were, he said there weren't any. I don't understand.'

'He probably didn't want to talk about it. Maybe if you ask him tomorrow he'll explain. Lights out at eight-thirty sharp, now, remember.'

Sarah forgot about the dragonflies and started reading instead.

Two doors along the hall, Tom was showing the dragon his picture of Dragonrise. The dragon seemed to like it. In fact he puffed out so much hot air when he was looking at it that Tom had to put the picture back up on the wall in a hurry to prevent it going up in smoke.

'A truly magnificent picture. Superb. It gives me a strange feeling somewhere here.' The dragon laid one set of red claws against the shiny diamond-shaped scales of his chest. 'I'm amazed you didn't get two gold stars.'

There was no doubt about it, thought Tom. The dragon knew a good work of art when he saw it, even if he couldn't paint or draw himself. 'Claws too long,' he explained, with a touch of regret. 'When I curl them round a paintbrush I end up cutting myself. The paper goes all green and bloody before I even start.'

'Tell me some more about dragons, and then I can draw the pictures for you.'

One thing a dragon likes almost as much as fighting and feasting is talking, so Tom's proposal was very much to the dragon's taste.

'Dragons,' he began in a voice that made Tom think of Mrs Steel, 'are the most ancient creatures to be found upon the face of the earth, or any other part of the earth for that matter. According to legend, they were first known in China seven trillennia ago, give or take a year. No one knows how these first dragons spread westwards. Some say they ran – and it is true that a dragon may travel well over two thousand miles in a week. Some say they sailed in dragon boats, lashing the water with their tails to drive their craft onwards. Some suggest that these first dragons flew west – even that they were not hatched in China at all, but flew there out of the night itself. I myself –' but here the dragon hesitated.

'Go on. How do you think the dragons travelled west?'

From the way the dragon cleared his throat, he seemed to want to change the subject, but Tom overruled him.

'Well, I believe – it's just a theory, mark you, although some interesting evidence is coming to light that supports me –'

'How?' Tom insisted pointedly.

The dragon took a deep breath. 'Through the tunnels of fire,' he said impressively. 'The paths that lead through the fiery heart of the earth, from north to south and from east to west. Nowadays, of course, the tunnels have shrivelled and disappeared from view, but in the first dragon days things may have been very different. Dragons have always loved fire, and sought darkness. What could be more natural than for our Chinese ancestors to have found a way into the dark passages that wind beneath the earth's surface and to have followed them to the earth's core and on, up and out again?' The dragon's green eyes shone. 'And that would explain why the dragons in the West are generally so much smaller than those that stayed behind in China. Our ancestors would have had to be small to thread their way through the underground tunnels. Large dragons couldn't have made it. It all fits, you see. What do you say?'

'It must have taken them an awfully long time to get from one side to the other.'

'Oh, a hundred years or more, at a guess.'

Tom looked thoughtful. 'What do you think they could have eaten on the way?'

For once a hint of impatience crept into the dragon's response. 'That's not the important part of the story. What does it matter whether they ate worms, or moles, or took corned beef sandwiches?' He snorted in a way that ought to have warned Tom, but didn't.

'I was just wondering. And what would they have had to drink, do you suppose?'

'Coca-cola, I expect,' said the dragon, fearfully annoyed. 'Who cares? Do you never think of anything but food and drink?'

Coming from a dragon who had always seemed to attach great importance to feasting, this was a little unreasonable, but Tom saw that it would be better to keep his doubts to himself. 'You did ask what I thought,' he said, with some reproach.

The dragon had been gazing stiffly at the bedroom curtains, but now he turned a chilly look in Tom's direction.

'It's my own fault, I suppose. You are too young to understand the beauty of ancient dragon lore. No, don't apologize –' (Tom hadn't been going to, but now he hurriedly said, 'I'm sorry.') 'We will never refer to the incident again. I tell you what,' he went on, brightening, 'I'll adopt you as my blood brother to show there are no hard feelings. Give me your hand.'

Tom obeyed, with the private wish that the dragon would watch what he did with his claws. With his left front paw, the dragon gently pressed the palm of Tom's hand. The paw felt warm, like a hot water bottle. 'Do just what I do.'

Putting on a saintly expression which Tom privately

thought overdone but did his best to copy, the dragon said solemnly:

> 'Claw to claw in peace and war.
> Scale to scale will never fail.

Go on, now you say it.'

> 'Claw to claw in peace and war.
> Scale to scale will never fail.'

As Tom repeated the words, the dragon gave Tom's hand three squeezes, and Tom did his best to give three squeezes back, although the paw didn't squeeze easily.

'There. That makes us dragon brothers to the death.' The dragon had completely recovered his temper, to Tom's relief. 'Now it's time for you to go to bed, or people will start knocking on your door to complain.'

'I'll see you again tomorrow?' It wasn't really a question. By now Tom felt sure the dragon would be coming back.

'May I go to Wales if you don't,' said the dragon, disappearing underneath the bed. 'See you at Dragon-rise.'

Chapter Four

On Wednesday morning, Mrs Steel asked Tom's class to do some writing for her. Each child had to write about his favourite animal.

'And *not* your dog or your cat, please,' she said. 'Try to think of something really interesting.'

Later on, as she looked through what the children had written, Mrs Steel gave a sigh. It was just as she had expected. There were four goldfish, six hamsters, eight gerbils, three guinea-pigs, two parrots, five mice and one dragon.

One dragon?

She picked up the last sheet of paper again.

'Dragons are green,' she read. 'They are quite small. They have spyckes along thier backs and red clors. Thier skin is skaly. They can breeth fire but they ar'nt suppose to. They like nigth best. They came from China long agow. I like dragons because they are good to talk too.'

Mrs Steel smiled. Then she laughed. This was certainly better than goldfish. She shut her eyes to the spelling and gave Tom another star.

She also went out after school to find Tom's mother in the playground where all the parents waited for their children at going-home time. When Mrs Smith saw

Tom's teacher coming, her heart sank. If a teacher wants to talk to a parent, it usually means trouble. But this time everything was all right. Mrs Steel only wanted to say what nice work Tom had been doing lately, and to ask the name of the book about dragons that Mrs Smith had been reading to Tom at home; she thought it might be suitable to read aloud to the class at story-time.

'Dragons?' Mrs Smith looked puzzled. 'I have been reading *Winnie the Pooh* to him. But I don't think dragons came into that. Are you sure you don't mean tigers? Or kangaroos?'

Mrs Steel was quite sure.

'Then Tom must have been hearing about dragons from someone else. Perhaps there's been something about them on the television.'

Mrs Steel and Mrs Smith both looked inquiringly at Tom. He looked down at his toes with a modest smile, saying nothing.

'I expect that's the answer,' agreed Mrs Steel, when the pause had lasted several seconds. 'The children's programmes are excellent these days.'

'Mighty Mouse is the best,' said Tom. Luckily for him, Sarah ran up before Mrs Steel could say what she thought about cartoons. His mother said goodbye to the teacher politely and they set off home.

At Dragonrise that night, Tom noticed that the dragon seemed unusually excited. Instead of settling down comfortably on the eiderdown for a talk, he twitched his tail from side to side every few seconds, blowing showers of sparks, like tiny red sequins, from his nose.

'I think we'd do better on the floor tonight,' Tom suggested at last. 'I don't know how I could explain things to Mummy if I get holes burnt in my eiderdown. You're very fiery. Is something the matter?'

The dragon climbed, not down to the floor but up onto the windowsill. 'A dragon can't help but be fiery on a night like this.' He swept the curtains apart with an eager paw, and flattened his nose against the glass. 'Just look at that sky.' As he gazed up in rapture at the inky blackness, he let out a windy sigh that made the glass in the windowpane seethe and bubble.

'Stop,' cried Tom in dismay, flinging the window wide open. A hole in the glass would be even worse than one in the eiderdown. 'You must be more careful or we'll get into trouble.'

The dragon looked a little guilty, but not for long. 'It's the dark of the moon. The sight of a black sky always takes a dragon that way, Tom. It's in our blood, I'm afraid. I tell you what: we'll go up and sit on the roof instead of staying cooped up in here. Then it won't matter how excited I get.'

'On the roof? I could never get up there.'

'It's easy. Just hold onto my tail and we'll be off.'

Tom began to say that he was very sorry but of course he could do no such thing because his parents were not in favour of children climbing on the roof at night, or even in the day – but the dragon was already half out of the window.

'Come back,' cried Tom in panic, making a grab at the green tail.

Then suddenly he wasn't leaning on the windowsill any longer: he was clinging to something green and

scaly that hung over the edge of the guttering above the bedroom window. He hardly had time to feel surprised at this – and no time at all to feel scared – before he was sitting up on the ridge of the roof with the dragon beside him.

It was a moment or two before he could remember how his voice worked. 'How ... how did we get here?' he managed to say, after swallowing hard.

The dragon held out his paw, palm up, in explanation. 'Suction pads. They stick onto things,' he said, seeing that Tom was still staring at him round-eyed. He tapped one of the small round bobbles that could be seen growing near the bottom of the sharp, bright claws. 'If I use these I can hold onto almost anything. Gutters and drainpipes are easy. I could walk up the outside of the Empire State Building if I wanted to.'

Tom shuddered. A two-storey house was bad enough to find yourself on top of unexpectedly. Anything higher didn't bear thinking about.

'As it happens,' the dragon went on cheerfully, 'I can think of few places I would less like to be. Dragons do not, in general, care for great heights. However, in some emergency such as –' he paused, trying and failing to hit on the kind of emergency where climbing up the Empire State Building might be the only thing for a sensible dragon to do '– in some emergency, I could be up there in two flicks of a dragon's tail.'

Tom had more immediate things on his mind. 'Now we're up on the roof,' he said, cautiously loosening one set of fingers from the ridge tile he had been clutching, 'what do we do?'

'We examine the heavens,' replied the dragon.

Tom looked up obediently. At once he gave a gasp of delight. The sky arched above him like an upturned bowl, sprinkled with faint points of light. A soft wind ruffled his hair. He could hear it stirring the leaves of the old beech that grew beside the house. The air smelt of grass and leaves and the currant bushes budding in the back garden below him. 'It's beautiful.'

'It's one of the most beautiful sights on this earth,' agreed the dragon, with great seriousness. 'When I look at these stars, the names of dragons who were dust ten centuries ago and more come back into my mind. Dragons whose fire was quenched before I ever hatched once sat watching these same stars at the dark of the moon, drinking the dark as we do. It gives me a strange feeling just here' – the dragon patted his stomach – 'almost as if I were hungry. By the way,' he added casually, 'which room did you say belonged to your sister Sarah?'

'It's next door to the bathroom.' Tom was still gazing at the sky above in wonder.

'And that is ...?' The dragon rose just as casually to his feet.

'Just over there,' answered Tom, with a vague wave of his hand, his thoughts still a million miles away among the stars.

'Thank you.' The dragon's voice was full of satisfaction. 'If you'll just excuse me for a moment, I won't be long.'

'Where are you going?' asked Tom, coming back to real life with a start. 'If you wake Sarah up you'll get into awful trouble. She'll tell Mummy. Sarah tells Mummy *everything*.'

'She won't tell her about me,' the dragon pleaded. 'I can guarantee it.'

'No.'

The dragon didn't look convinced, so Tom caught hold of him by the tail to be on the safe side. It was almost the worst thing he could have done. Taken by surprise, the dragon staggered backwards. For one dreadful moment it seemed as if both he and Tom were going to slide right off the roof. The suction pads saved them in the nick of time. Tom heard a tile crash down onto the path below, then the night air was rushing by him and he was suddenly back inside his bedroom again.

The dragon looked almost as flustered as Tom. 'Give me a little warning the next time you do that. We almost brought the chimney down with us.'

'I didn't want you to leave me alone up there,' Tom explained. 'And you *must* keep out of Sarah's way. She'll spoil everything.'

'But I *told* you ...' the dragon began. Then he saw the obstinate look on Tom's face and gave up. 'Oh very well, we'll say no more about it.'

It wasn't exactly the promise Tom had been hoping for.

He offered the dragon a gobstopper, as a way of making up for the shock he'd given him. The offer was accepted, but the dragon looked as if his mind was on other things.

As Tom fell asleep, he had a hazy idea that the

dragon was reciting to himself again, from his usual post underneath the bed. For the sake of Tom's peace of mind, it was perhaps a good thing that for once the dragon was mumbling.

> 'Whoever would have missed her,
> That awful Sarah sister?'

he concluded moodily.

For a long time after Tom's eyes were shut fast, the dragon's green eyes could be seen glittering in the gloom as if he were thinking hungry thoughts.

Chapter Five

Over breakfast the next morning Tom thought about what dragons like to eat. It seemed possible that problems lay ahead.

On the one hand, dragons will be dragons. You can't expect a creature that breathes fire and regularly appears from nowhere underneath your bed to live on a diet of gobstoppers. Or even cornflakes, he reflected, taking another spoonful.

'Don't chew with your mouth open,' said Sarah. 'I can see all your food slurping around. Yughh.'

On the other hand, a diet of what dragons like best was out of the question. For one thing, what would the dragon do about the bones? You couldn't just leave them lying about, or put them out for the dustmen with the other rubbish. And what about the victim's clothes? Would the dragon eat them too?

Tom eyed Sarah thoughtfully.

She paused in the act of spreading a thick layer of honey on top of her toast. 'Don't you know it's rude to stare at people? You don't know *anything*. Mummy, Tom's being rude.'

There were six buttons on Sarah's blouse. Tom counted them. There were two on her pinafore as well. They didn't look as if they would be pleasant to eat.

No, the dragon was bound not to want to swallow her clothes. They would have to be got rid of somehow, too. As a meal, even more than as a sister, Sarah would have serious drawbacks.

What was the best way of explaining this to a hungry dragon?

'Hurry up, Tom, or you'll be late for school.' It was Tom's father speaking. It was no wonder he sounded impatient. He was trying to drink coffee, shut his brief-case, eat a piece of toast and leaf through the telephone directory all at the same time. 'Who did we get to mend the gutter last year?' he called to Tom's mother, who was in the kitchen. 'How that tile got knocked down last night I can't imagine. I said *hurry up*, Tom. It isn't as though it was even a windy night.' He found a number and began to dial as Tom, a little guiltily, went upstairs.

On the way out of the house five minutes later he stopped to give his father a special hug.

'I'm sorry about the tile.'

His father laughed. 'That's all right, Tom. It's not your fault that it happened.'

That's true, thought Tom, getting into the car. It was more the dragon's fault than mine. That still left untouched, however, the problems of what dragons eat.

Tom thought about this on and off all day, and by the time he got home from school he had had an idea. When his mother went out to weed the garden after tea, Tom sneaked into the kitchen.

First he took a small plastic wastebin bag from the

drawer. Then he got to work He tackled the re-
frigerator first.

Into the bag went:
a square of butter
a corner of cheese
a carrot
three lettuce leaves
a chunk of cucumber
half a tomato
a spoonful of raw minced beef
a frozen fish finger (from the freezer)

Two slices of wholemeal bread went in on top, and
Tom was just wondering about a raw potato, or pos-
sibly a dollop of tomato ketchup when disaster struck.
Sarah walked in.

'What have you got in there?' She pointed suspiciously to the bulging bag. Tom tried to hide it, too
late. Sarah pounced and had the bag open before he
could think of any way to stop her. She wrinkled her
face up at the sight of what was inside it.

'What on earth do you want all that for?'

'It's an experiment.' Tom had often found this a
useful all-purpose excuse. You could get away with
almost anything in pursuit of science. It didn't work
with Sarah, though.

'What sort of an experiment?'

'It's a secret.'

'Are you allowed to take all those bits of food?'

Tom knew what was coming next. It did.

'I'm going to tell Mummy,' said Sarah.

'You'll be sorry if you do.' Tom was getting very

annoyed. 'If I don't carry out this experiment, you're for it.'

'What do you mean?' Sarah paused, puzzled, on her way to the door.

Tom glared at her. 'The experiment's for *you*,' he shouted.

Her eyes widened. Tom didn't usually do things for her, experiments or anything else. 'Is it really? Cross your heart?'

Tom nodded, still glaring.

'All right. If you're doing it for me, I won't tell.'

Sarah went out, quietly for her. Tom heaved a sigh of relief and took himself off upstairs. The bag went under his pillow. He wanted to give the dragon a surprise.

It was a surprise, too. When Tom brought the bag triumphantly out of its hiding place, the dragon looked quite taken aback.

'Mmm. Interesting,' he said, taking a cautious sniff at the fish finger, then withdrawing rapidly. 'What do you do with it?'

'*I* don't do anything with it,' said Tom gleefully. 'It's for you. You *eat* it.'

The dragon opened his mouth as if to speak, then shut it again. He couldn't help feeling touched by Tom's thoughtfulness. But friendship must draw the line somewhere, surely? He watched uneasily as Tom took the contents of the bag out one by one and spread them out invitingly.

'There's even some salad,' Tom explained, his eyes shining. The dragon regarded the lettuce leaves without noticeable enthusiasm. 'The brown bits don't matter.

You hardly taste them if you don't chew too much. I'll wipe the butter off the carrot for you.'

The dragon stifled a shudder as Tom transferred the butter from the carrot to the fish finger.

'There,' Tom finished, when the whole menu was spread out before him. 'What are you going to have first?'

The dragon looked from the food to his friend's delighted face. His heart sank, but he steeled himself to do what must be done. 'My, oh my, I hardly know where to begin,' he said, in a hearty voice. 'It's all so tempting. Perhaps I should leave some for tomorrow?' He looked at Tom hopefully, but Tom shook his head.

'It'll go off if we leave it inside the bag for a whole day,' he pointed out. 'It would be an awful shame if we had to throw it away.'

'It would? I mean, it would, wouldn't it.' The dragon took a deep breath and put the piece of cheese on top of the fish finger, sandwiched these between the bread, piled mince, tomato and cucumber on top, and viewed the result doubtfully. 'Do you by any chance have a gobstopper?' he asked, turning to Tom.

Tom produced one from his pocket. The dragon removed most of the fluff from it, and put it on top of the mince. 'To take the taste away – I mean, to bring out the flavour,' he said.

Then he put the whole lot in his mouth, shut his eyes and swallowed it at one gulp.

He opened his eyes a few seconds later to find Tom watching him expectantly.

'That was delicious,' said the dragon. At least he made a gallant attempt to say it. All that came out

was a kind of moan. He tried again. 'Delicious,' he croaked. Then he shut his eyes and put his head down on the eiderdown.

'Have the carrot, too,' Tom urged.

'No, I'll save it for later.'

'Are you sure you've had enough?'

'Oh yes.' The dragon's eyes were still shut tight. He looked to Tom like someone doing a complicated piece of arithmetic in his head.

Presently he opened one eye. Its expression was profoundly sad. 'I think the gobstopper went down the wrong way. If you don't mind, I think I'll just lie on the floor under the bed for a while.'

'Of course I don't mind,' said Tom. Disappointment

should never make you impolite. 'I hope you feel better soon.'

The dragon clambered stiffly off the bed and vanished from sight.

'I don't think I've ever felt like this before.' His voice floated up through the mattress. 'I must have a delicate stomach.'

Later on he said, more mournfully still, 'It reminds me of Wales.' Tom didn't answer him, for the excellent reason that he was already fast asleep.

Chapter Six

Friday was the best day of the week for Tom. The weekend lay just ahead, with no school and the possibility of soccer with his friends, trips to Wetherburn Common to play cowboys and indians, and a visit to the toyshop to spend his Saturday pocket money.

First, however, he had to get through Friday. Under

Mrs Steel's eye, this was never easy. It was harder than usual when he had an evening with the dragon to think about, as well as all the regular weekend pleasures.

That day Mrs Steel wrote a list of animals up on the blackboard.

'I want you to split these animals into two groups,' she told the children. 'Put the farm animals in one list, and the wild animals in another.'

'Farm animals,' Tom wrote carefully. 'Pig, horse, sheep.' His mind began to wander. He copied the next three animals straight off the list on the board. 'Hyena, giraffe, bear.'

When she read Tom's answers, Mrs Steel was not amused. 'Try harder,' she wrote at the foot of the page. 'Why ever would a farmer want to keep a hyena?'

During the maths class, Tom thought of several answers.

The farmer might just like hyenas.

Hyenas might frighten the rabbits off the corn.

Hyenas might eat slugs, or wild oats.

They might help the farmer to guess what the weather was going to be by twitching their ears when rain was coming.

Naturally you can't think about a question as complicated as this and do your maths as fast as normal.

'Why didn't you finish?' wrote Mrs Steel in big red letters at the bottom of Tom's sheet of answers.

Tom said he'd been thinking about hyenas. It wasn't a good answer in Mrs Steel's opinion. Tom had to stay in to do the rest of the maths problems when the other children were playing.

It was a pretty typical Friday, in fact, only a little worse.

The dragon was more than sympathetic. When Tom told him about Mrs Steel his eyes lit up like birthday-cake candles.

'How old is this teacher of yours? It's possible that I might be able to give you a hand with her.'

Tom had never thought about Mrs Steel's age before. Closely questioned by the dragon, he ended up giving the opinion that Mrs Steel would *not* count as a damsel, girl or maiden.

The warm glow in the dragon's eyes faded. 'I couldn't eat her then, I'm afraid. What a pity.'

'Oh, she's not *that* bad,' said Tom hastily. The dragon's way of solving problems was a bit extreme. 'Tell me some more about dragons, will you? There's lots I don't understand. For instance, where do you go during the day? Before Dragonrise, I mean.'

He was sorry as soon as he'd said it. After one swift glance at Tom's face, the dragon turned to look out between the curtains at the dark sky. When he spoke, his voice was quiet.

'It's a long story. Long and sad. When the world was young, the power of the dragon was strong. We loved the darkness that fed our flames, but the light of the sun could not harm us. We often slept through the day, in tunnels or caves for preference, but we had no need to hide. Then, as the earth's fires cooled, our power grew weak. Some dragons found the sun's light so painful that they went underground for ever. Those that did not, and I was one of them, have to suffer the fading. In the full light of day we simply disappear. It doesn't hurt,' he added, catching a glimpse of Tom's face reflected in the glass. 'Fading protects us. It's sad only because it is a sign of our ageing.'

Looking far out into the night, he went on, as if to himself or to someone Tom couldn't see.

'Come my brother, come my friend,
All good things must reach an end.
We will shrink not, though we fade.
Face the daylight unafraid.

Let the sun unloose its darts:
It will never daunt our hearts.
Face the daylight undismayed,
Dragons still, although we fade.'

Tom wanted to say something to make the dragon feel better, but he couldn't find the right words. It was hard to see how something as solid, as warm and strong as the dragon could just vanish away in the light of day. As it happened, the dragon was rarely sad for long. While Tom was still wondering whether or not dragons liked to be hugged, and what the risks were of tearing his pyjamas if he tried, the dragon spun round to face him.

'Why waste the night in regrets?' he said, his eyes gleaming. 'I've a better story for you. It's about the time I rescued a young friend of mine called Gawain – you remind me of him, actually – from a ravening octo-cat.'

'Octo-what?' asked Tom. 'I've heard of an octo*pus* but never of an octo*cat*.'

'Oh, octopuses are child's play to fully grown octocats. They have eight heads as well as eight arms, and eight eyes on each head, and eight claws on each arm – and so forth. Frightful creatures altogether. I can't advise you strongly enough to steer clear of them. Young Gawain, of course, ignored my warnings. Tried to steal one of the octocat's eggs for his egg collection. Luckily it all took place around Dragonrise and I was able to leap to his defence in the nick of time. It was nip and tuck for an hour or so, and then young Gawain crawled in under the octocat when she was concentrating on squeezing my head off, and finished her off with a stab from his pocket knife, right through the heart.'

'So *he* rescued *you*?' said Tom, trying to get things straight.

There was a slight pause.

The dragon raised his eyebrows. 'I suppose you might say that, if you wish utterly to distort the truth. Gawain made much the same sort of mistake, but I overlooked it. Errors of judgement made in the heat of a life-and-death struggle with an octocat are excusable. I was gathering my powers to wreak a hideous vengeance on the monster at the instant Gawain struck. The outcome was never in doubt.'

Tom said he saw that now, and apologized for having misunderstood. He was never quite sure why he asked the next question – it might just have been to introduce a new topic to distract the offended dragon, or it might have been something a lot more significant. Anyway, he suddenly found himself asking innocently, 'Did Gawain have a sister?'

The dragon started and gave Tom a wary look. 'In a sense,' was his reply, after a distinct pause.

'What sense?'

The dragon thought for a while. 'He did and he didn't.'

'I don't understand.'

The dragon gazed up at the ceiling. 'Well, first he *had* a sister,' he explained reluctantly. 'And then, quite suddenly, he *didn't*. Just one of those things.'

'What happened to her?'

'People,' said the dragon, choosing his words with some care, 'people never discovered. She might have run away to sea. She might have gone off to be a missionary. She might have been eaten by an octocat.'

Or by something else, thought Tom. But if the dragon knew, he clearly wasn't telling. It was time to change the subject.

'I've been wondering how old you are, Dragon. I know you're more than five hundred and one, because that's when your birthday feast was. How old are you now?'

'Not very old at all, really,' said the dragon, relaxing. It was tiring to have to keep a watch on your tongue as he'd had to over the matter of Gawain's sister – a female without a single redeeming feature, so far as he could remember. If you didn't count her plumpness, that was.

'At my last birthday I was eight thousand, seven hundred and fifty-four. You can tell roughly by looking at my spikes. Count how many I have on my spine.'

Tom knelt up beside the dragon and counted out loud, touching each brilliant green triangle as he spoke.

'One, two, three, four, five, six, seven, eight, nine –

or doesn t this one count?' he asked, his finger pausing on a middle-sized bump near the tail.

'That will be my next spike, and it won't be fully formed for another two hundred and forty-six years. One spike every thousand years, you see. And stop doing that – it tickles.'

Tom stopped stroking the bump. He could see that it was less scaly than the other spikes, which probably explained its ticklishness.

'About Gawain's sister,' he began. 'What do *you* think happ—' He stopped because the dragon was coughing violently. You don't get to be eight thousand, seven hundred and fifty-four without learning how to avoid awkward situations.

'Are you all right?' asked Tom with concern.

'Just a touch of my old trouble.' He patted his chest with one paw and coughed again. 'Nothing serious, but I'll have to stop talking. Don't worry about it.'

'What a shame. I had lots more things to ask you. Do you really have to go?'

The dragon coughed and nodded, accepted a gob-stopper to soothe his throat, and disappeared beneath the bed before Tom could ask anything else. The coughing, Tom was glad to hear, stopped almost at once.

It was not until he awoke next morning that Tom realized that, what with one thing and another, he had completely forgotten to ask what dragons like to eat *second* best. It was a matter, something inside warned him, that would have to be dealt with soon.

Chapter Seven

On Saturday morning, Tom and Sarah went with their parents to do the weekly shopping. As they went round the supermarket, Tom kept his eyes open for food that might interest a dragon. It was very difficult.

Take vegetables, for a start. Tom couldn't convince himself that a dragon with a taste for girls was going to look with much enthusiasm at cabbage or cauliflower. The same went for carrots – however good for the scales. Chips might be better, but how could Tom organize cooking them?

Tom's mother paused in front of the meat counter.

'What shall we get for Sunday lunch?' she asked Tom. Secretly she was amazed at the interest he was taking in choosing food. He was being especially good if you compared him with Sarah, who hated food shopping and had already had to be bribed with a stick of bubblegum to silence her complaints. 'Shall we have chicken? Or a shoulder of lamb? Or what about a joint of pork?'

This required serious thought. The sort of meat that a dragon would like would have to taste rather like Sarah. It was a pity that he couldn't see what she looked like inside. Would she be a pale colour like chicken, or a dark brown, like roast lamb? He looked at her with narrowed eyes. At that moment Sarah blew an enormous pink bubble, and then popped it with her tongue, making a noise like a balloon bursting.

If Sarah were an animal, thought Tom, what would she be? Not a chicken, certainly not a lamb ... Suddenly the answer came to him.

'Can we have pork for dinner tomorrow?' he asked his mother.

She bought the pork, and a lot of other things, until the trolley was almost too heavy to push. Tom went on being good for the rest of the trip. He was concentrating on how best to hide some of his Sunday lunch, and thinking how pleased the dragon would be when he tasted the Sarah-substitute.

Sarah went on blowing bubbles and popping them. There's no doubt about it, thought Tom as he watched her, pork was the right thing to choose.

That evening Tom told the dragon that he would be getting another surprise the following day.

'Let me guess,' the dragon said, shutting his eyes so tightly that the scales along his forehead buckled and squeaked. 'Don't tell me, don't tell me ...'

'I'm not going to,' promised Tom.

The dragon's eyes flew open. 'I know. It's a ... a football.'

Tom laughed and said, 'No.' The eyes snapped shut again.

'Don't tell me, don't tell me ...'

'I won't.'

'It's a ... a firework?' With his one open eye, the dragon saw Tom shake his head again, smiling.

'You'll never guess.'

The dragon sighed and unfurrowed his forehead to fix a pleading gaze on Tom's face. 'I give up then. What is it?'

'Wait and see. It's a *surprise*.'

'Yes, I know that. But I like to know what my surprises are going to be,' the dragon explained. 'It helps me get ready for them.'

Tom relented a little. 'I'll give you a clue, but that's all. It's something nice to eat. Not,' he added in a hurry, in case the dragon got the wrong idea, 'not what you like best. But something nice.'

The dragon looked hard at Tom, out of the corner of his eyes, which is impossible to do if you aren't a dragon, and makes you look extremely strange even if you are. 'It wouldn't by any chance be another – what was that thing you gave me to eat the other night? – another sandwich, would it? The nice surprise, I mean.'

Tom reassured him. The surprise was going to be much tastier than the sandwich.

That, thought the dragon, would not be difficult. Finding something *less* tasty than the sandwich would be the challenge. Even so, he cheered up. Following his own train of thought, he said in a careless voice, 'While we're on the subject of surprises, didn't you once tell me you had a sister?'

Tom knew perfectly well that the dragon knew perfectly well about Sarah, and he gave his friend a look full of suspicion. 'What's Sarah got to do with surprises?'

You eat surprises and you eat sisters, thought the

dragon, trying hard to look harmless. What could be simpler than that?

He didn't speak out loud, however, because Tom's disapproving gaze made him feel guilty. He could see that it might have been a mistake to introduce the subject of Sarah as he had. He had spoken without thinking, and was sorry for it.

'How was football this afternoon?' It was a lucky question for the dragon to hit on, just as the silence was threatening to turn awkward. Tom's expression brightened.

'Didn't I tell you? We drew, nil-nil, so we get one whole point. Are you sure I didn't tell you about it before?'

'Quite sure,' lied the dragon. He much preferred hearing Tom's account of the day's play again to discussing difficult topics such as a dragon's diet and its relation to young female relatives.

Ten minutes passed happily; then just as Tom was showing the dragon the proper way to head a football (using the pillow as an example), a movement above his head brought him to a sudden standstill.

'Ugh. Look up there, Dragon. It's a spider.'

The dragon looked. 'So it is.'

Tom didn't want the dragon to get the wrong idea, so he said at once that he wasn't frightened of spiders.

'Oh no,' answered the dragon readily. 'Neither am I.'

'But –' Tom sat down on the edge of his bed and looked up with narrowed eyes '– but I don't exactly *like* them.'

'Some people don't,' replied the dragon in a pleasant voice. 'Nothing to be ashamed of in not liking them. Lots of people don't.'

Tom became even more thoughtful. 'If someone, someone who didn't mind spiders, were to put that one out of the window, that would make the whole room sort of feel better. Do you see?'

'I can certainly see your point of view. Who could you get to do it, though?'

'Well … I thought maybe *you* could do it for me, dragon.'

The dragon stiffened slightly. 'Me?'

'Well, you're not frightened of a little spider, are you? I expect you could sleep in a whole room full of spiders and not give it a second thought. I wish I was a dragon.'

There was a short pause. 'I'm not *frightened* of spiders,' said the dragon, who had turned a little yellow at the mention of a roomful of them. 'Not frightened, exactly. No dragon is frightened of spiders. However, some dragons like them and some dragons don't. And *I* am one of the ones that don't,' he finished firmly.

'It's nothing to be ashamed of,' said Tom, who could see the dragon's position only too well. 'I wish the spider would stay still, that's all.'

'Yes,' said the dragon from underneath the bed.

Tom was too busy keeping an eye on the ceiling even to notice his friend's departure. 'I think I'll just go and ask Daddy to get rid of it for us. I wouldn't like it to fall off the ceiling.'

'It might hurt itself,' agreed the dragon in a muffled voice. 'I'll just keep out of the way until the thing's settled.'

Outside his bedroom door, Tom bumped into Sarah, who was on her way to the bathroom for a glass of water.

'You're supposed to be asleep,' she pointed out.

Tom explained his problem.

'Oh, I'll put it out for you,' Sarah said carelessly. 'I don't mind spiders. Where is it?'

Tom showed her. 'And don't touch it till I'm out of the way.'

Sarah gave him a pitying look, and went to fetch the bathroom chair to stand on and a face flannel (which Tom was glad to see wasn't his). She got into position beneath the spider.

'This is how you do it,' she said. 'First you put the flannel over your hand, like this. Then, very carefully, so you don't scare him, you put the flannel over the spider and – eeeghh.'

The directions ended suddenly as the spider made a rapid dash for the wall, closely pursued by the face flannel, with the result that Sarah and the flannel and the spider all came down in a tangle on the floor.

The spider set off briskly for the shelter of the shadow under Tom's bed, but Sarah was too quick for it.

'Ah.' She pounced, and picked it up by one black leg. 'It's really easier without the flannel if you don't mind how they feel. There it goes.' The spider went out through the bedroom window.

Sarah turned back to Tom. 'Spiders can't hurt you, you know, so it's silly to be a baby about them. That strange noise you made when it tried to run under the bed almost put me off.'

'I didn't –' Tom began, but he thought better of it.

When Sarah had gone, he told the dragon it was safe to come out again. It was quite a while before he emerged, and when he did so, Tom looked at him with surprise.

'Are you all right?' If he hadn't known that dragons are green, he would have described his friend at this point as definitely yellow. The voice matched the colouring, weak and shaky.

'Just give me a few minutes. Did you see that spider coming for me? My whole life passed before my eyes in an instant. I almost cried out –'

'You *did* cry out.'

'And then everything went dark. Did she – ugh, I can scarcely bear to ask – pick it up?'

'She did.' Tom and the dragon looked at each other silently.

'With her bare hands?'

Tom nodded and shuddered at the same time.

'And it's really gone?'

'She dropped it out of the window.'

The dragon thought for a while and finally shook his head. 'I feel a little weak still, so, if you don't mind, I shall retire early.' He looked hard into the gloom of the area beneath the bed. There didn't seem to be anything small and leggy lurking there. He disappeared.

As Tom was falling asleep, the dragon spoke again.

'Is the window tightly shut?'

'Yes,' Tom answered without opening his eyes.

'Are you *sure*?'

'I've checked it twice.'

'That's all right then,' said the dragon. 'You can't be too careful with spiders.'

Then they both fell asleep.

Chapter Eight

The following day was one Tom remembered for a long time. It was pretty important for Sarah, too, although she never realized it.

The day began just like any other Sunday, with both children eating their breakfast in front of the television. It was a Sunday treat to be allowed to do this without getting dressed. It was just bad luck that it led to the first of the day's mishaps.

Sarah always enjoyed switching the television set on and off. As soon as the programme was finished, she jumped up to get to the set. By accident, she trod on Tom's foot on the way.

'Ow,' said Tom, more cross than hurt. 'Don't switch off. I want to hear the music they play at the end.'

But Sarah had already pressed the off-button. Before she could switch on again, Tom leapt to his feet with a howl of rage, forgetting the full bowl of cereal on his knee. Cornflakes and milk soared through the air and landed all over the television set, the carpet and Sarah.

'Look what you've done,' shouted Sarah.

'It was your fault.'

Sarah burst into angry tears and made a dash for the door. Tom saw at once that she was going to go

and tell his parents a lot of lies about what had just taken place, so he set off for the door only an instant later. He was a bit nearer to it than Sarah, so they ended up colliding. Sarah won, because she was bigger.

'You've hurt my shoulder,' Tom shouted up the stairs after her. 'Pig.'

When he reached his parents' bedroom Sarah was sobbing out a story about Tom throwing his breakfast all over her. Tom began to explain how it had all been Sarah's fault in the first place.

Neither of the parents was particularly pleased. Sarah was told to go and find a cloth to clear up the milk, Tom to pick up every single stray cornflake.

'You're always on Tom's side,' Sarah cried, bursting into tears again at the unfairness of it all.

'Why do I always get the worst job?' shouted Tom, no better pleased.

'Don't let me hear another word out of either of you until you've got that room cleared up,' snapped their father.

'And do go and pick the cornflakes out of your hair, darling,' called their mother to Sarah as they left.

It wasn't an ideal start to the day.

Lunchtime saw things take a turn for the worse.

Tom had worked out a plan for how to save some roast pork to give to the dragon that evening. He set about carrying it out.

'Can I have a lot of pork, please, Mummy?'

'I want lots too,' said Sarah at once.

Their mother sighed and said that there was enough for everyone.

Tom took his plate and then – with regret, because

he really loved roast pork – put his elbow down heavily on the edge and flipped the meat onto the floor.

Sarah's mouth fell open with shock. 'Tom! Look what you've done.'

His mother sighed even harder. 'You can't eat that, now it's been on the floor. Pick it up and take it out to the bin in the kitchen. You can have a *little* more when you come back.'

So far so good. In the kitchen Tom bundled the meat into a strip of kitchen paper, and looked around for a good place to hide it until it could be collected safely later on. The breadbin seemed the best place: no one would be cutting any bread until suppertime at the earliest, so the parcel should be safe from discovery. Tom pushed the package into the back corner of the breadbin and went back to the dining room to have lunch. Everything seemed to have gone smoothly.

Later developments, however, included some Tom had not bargained for.

First, his mother decided to spend the afternoon baking in the kitchen. Every time Tom sneaked in to get the meat, he had to sneak out again empty-handed. By four o'clock he was hot and bothered, but at last his mother was clearing up. Tom heaved a sigh of relief. Soon the coast would be clear.

He hadn't taken into account Sarah, though. As soon as the clearing-up was done, Sarah asked if *she* could do some baking of her own.

'Come roller skating instead,' suggested Tom desperately. Perhaps he might be able to push her over and then rush back to get the meat from its hiding place before she recovered.

Sarah didn't even answer – the cornflakes had not been forgotten. She set off for the kitchen, with her mother's permission, and started getting out pots and pans, rolling pins and graters, bags of flour and bottles of food colouring.

Tom had another try. 'I want to do baking, too.' At least he could keep an eye on Sarah if he was in the kitchen with her.

'No,' said his father and mother at the same moment. 'There's been enough quarrelling for one day. You are going out into the garden for an hour to let Sarah do her baking in peace.'

Tom could tell that any more arguing was just going to get him into trouble. He gave in and went outside.

It was getting on for six o'clock before he had a chance to get the kitchen to himself. Sarah had gone, leaving a trail of flour and crumbs across the floor. The sound of the lawn-mower told him that his father was at work on the front lawn. He could see his mother away at the far end of the garden attacking the dandelions in the lettuce patch. It was the perfect opportunity. Tom went straight over to the breadbin and reached in for the parcel.

There was nothing there.

Tom couldn't believe it. He fetched a chair to stand on, and looked right down inside the bin. There was nothing but a small bit of loaf.

Upstairs, Sarah was moving about, singing. Tom went to the kitchen wastebin and looked inside. There, underneath a heap of flour and crumbs – crumbs? – was the paper he'd wrapped the pork in. But there was no meat. It had vanished completely.

Could his mother have ...? But she would have had no reason to open the breadbin, let alone to have hidden his parcel of pork.

His father? No better.

Sarah ...? Sarah ... The trail of breadcrumbs caught Tom's eye. It was like fitting a difficult piece into a jigsaw puzzle. He could almost *see* Sarah reaching down into the breadbin for some bread to grate into crumbs, finding the parcel, unwrapping it ... then what?

Tom could picture it only too well.

Without stopping to think, he raced upstairs to find her. 'What have you done with my pork?' he shouted.

Sarah looked innocent. 'What pork?'

'You've eaten it, you pig.'

'I don't know what you're talking about,' said Sarah, but her face went red.

Tom began to shout that he'd tell his mother what she'd done, but he realized in the middle of saying it that he couldn't even punish his sister by telling tales: not if it landed him with some awkward explaining of his own. 'I hate you,' he said, trying not to cry, and ran off to his own room.

'Who cares?' was Sarah's defiant reply. In fact she was feeling guilty, and it brought out the worst side of her nature.

Tom slammed his bedroom door and flung himself onto the bed. The disappointment over having no surprise to offer the dragon that night was hard to bear. And the question of what to give the dragon to eat was still unresolved.

Or was it?

Tom's thoughts returned to Sarah. It would be her own fault if the dragon ate *her*. Her own fault? It would be no more than simple justice. It wouldn't be his responsibility at all.

All at once, the decision was taken.

Which is how it happened that a few hours later Tom found himself telling the dragon that so far as the rules about eating sisters were concerned, things had changed dramatically. As of that moment, the dragon was welcome to fit Sarah into the menu as and when it suited him.

'And you won't mind?' asked the dragon, taken by surprise.

'Not a bit.' She shouldn't have been such a pig, thought Tom.

'You really and truly mean it? It's not a joke?'

'Cross my heart and hope to die.' You couldn't make it more solemn than that.

Overcome with emotion, the dragon held out a green sturdy paw to Tom, and Tom slipped his hand inside it.

'Claw to claw in peace and war,' recited the dragon in reverent tones.

'Scale to scale will never fail,' responded Tom seriously.

'That's that then. What we need now is a plan of action.'

Tom frowned. 'Can't you just go along now and eat her up?'

'Oh no, no, no,' said the dragon, shocked. 'That would never do. There are rules about how dragons handle these things. We aren't monsters.'

'What rules?'

'Tons and tons of them. You can't eat someone with an X in her name, for instance.' There was a brief pause while the dragon satisfied himself that this wouldn't put Sarah on the list of forbidden foods, then he continued briskly, 'Can't eat on the third Wednesday in February or the fourth Sunday in August –'

'Why ever not?'

'If you don't understand that, I'm afraid I can't help you. It's one of the things dragons know. An instinct. Can't eat when the wind's in the north-west. Can't eat in lots of situations, and one of them is when the meal

77

is a gift made less than twenty-four hours previously.
I imagine the council that drew up that rule was keen
to stamp out bad-mannered bolting. Whatever their
reason, there it is: I can't eat your generous surprise
until tomorrow evening at the earliest. And *then* if possible, I ought to approach the meal from the west, at
the instant of Dragonrise.'

Tom thought, while the dragon racked his brains
to remember which way was north and, failing that,
which way was west, without success.

'I know,' said Tom at last, just when the dragon
was showing signs of frustration. 'The sun shines in at
Sarah's window in the morning so it must face east.
So if you wait behind the currant bushes in the back
garden tomorrow evening, you'll be able to approach
from the west and get in through her bedroom window when Dragonrise comes. She always leaves her
window open, and you can just go straight up the
wall of the house on your suckers and climb in and
get her.'

The dragon considered the plan, and found it good.
In fact it was better than good: it met all the rules
about eating that he could remember. He bade Tom a
warm goodnight and retired early beneath the bed to
wait, with more than usual eagerness, for the coming
day.

You might imagine that Tom passed a sleepless
night, thinking of Sarah's approaching fate. If so, you
thought wrong. The day's disturbances had left him
tired, and he yawned as he listened to the dragon's
murmurings:

'Give me a dish that is ever new,
A maiden pie or a damsel stew.
Eaten slowly – nothing crude –
Swallowed only when well chewed,
That's the food that I *call* food.'

Filled with a sense of quiet satisfaction, he quickly fell asleep.

Chapter Nine

Mrs Steel liked to begin the week as she meant to go on, so Monday mornings were apt to be busy. As he wondered about the right way to spell write, and how anyone could be expected to take twenty-nine away from forty-five without first taking nine away from five, which everyone knows can't be done, Tom naturally had no time to brood.

At morning playtime he had a wrestling match with John Murphy, which ended in a muddy draw. It also ended with Tom spending the afternoon playtime inside in the classroom, in disgrace. The good thing about being in disgrace was that it meant he could have his favourite picture book about pirates all to himself for once, so Tom didn't mind that much about missing playtime. John Murphy, who had to make do with the story of a butterfly's life in pictures, and didn't like books anyway, minded much more.

In fact, for Tom the day passed just like any other, as really important days so often seem to. No wonder that by the time school was over, and Tom was curled up comfortably watching Mighty Mouse on the television, he had quite forgotten that after Dragonrise his life would never be the same again.

Sarah's day had been less satisfactory.

A new girl, Amanda Murray, had arrived in Sarah's class. Mr Elliot, the teacher, had given Sarah the job of looking after her and showing her around on her first day. That was fine: Sarah liked showing people what to do. Amanda was nice, too, which made it even better.

That was how the trouble started, really. Amanda was so nice that Sarah's best friend Lisa wanted to share the showing around. While Lisa and Sarah were arguing about who should show what, Amanda wandered off and started playing with Karen, who was not one of Sarah's friends at all – quite the opposite.

'I'm showing Amanda around,' Sarah told Karen. She took hold of Amanda's arm to prove her point.

'She doesn't want to play with *you*.' The face Karen made when she said this was quite horrible.

Sarah decided to ignore her, and turned away, taking Amanda's arm with her. Amanda would probably have followed, but before she could make up her mind, she was suddenly in the middle of a war.

Five minutes later they were all inside explaining to Mr Elliot what had happened. Or trying to explain.

Sarah was nursing a kicked ankle and Lisa looked as if she was going to get a black eye. Karen said she was going to be sick, so she missed most of the telling-off.

Sarah struggled hard not to cry, what with the kicked ankle and the unfairness of it all. Then Amanda squeezed her hand and smiled at her and she felt a little better.

However, back in class again, Sarah discovered that Amanda had been put on a more advanced maths problem book than she was on. What's more, Amanda finished before Sarah did. Later on she was given a reading text one book ahead of Sarah's, when before Sarah had been ahead of all the rest of the class.

Amanda knew what nine times eight was without thinking, and she could spell words Sarah didn't even know how to say.

So, while Sarah would have *liked* to like Amanda, it wasn't going to be easy.

On the way home she complained so much that life was unfair that in the end her mother lost patience. She sent Sarah out to weed the flowerbeds in the back garden as the only way to get a little peace.

There are worse things to do when you're feeling miserable than gardening. The earth was damp from

overnight rain, and Sarah's fingers pulled out chickweed and groundsel by the handful. Soon there were only dandelions left, harder to deal with because of their long tap roots. She decided that the best way to cope with them would be to scour out a hole round the root, working her fingers in as deep as she could, and then try to pull from as low down the root as possible. She settled down to work.

A few minutes later Tom heard the sound of a scream. He jumped up from his chair and ran over to the window.

It sounded like Sarah.

It was Sarah.

Curiosity took him outside to see what was the matter. He stopped a little way away from her, in case whatever it was was dangerous.

Sarah had stopped screaming, but she was shaking, her face all red and shiny with tears. 'Get Mummy,' she shouted. 'I've got a worm on me.'

'A what on you?'

'A *worm*. Don't just stand there. Go and get Mummy. And hurry!'

Tom looked at her in astonishment. 'Did you say a worm? Is that all?'

'It's on my sock, you dumbwit,' Sarah wailed in fury. 'I picked it up with the dandelion root, and when I shook it off my hand it dropped onto me again.'

Coming closer, Tom could see the worm. It was a healthy-looking specimen: at least six inches long, and a good wet pink colour. Considering what it had just been through, it was in fair shape.

He picked it up very gently and carried it to the back

of the flowerbed. The chickweed there was still thick enough to give a worm some place to hide. When he put it down it disappeared immediately.

'I think it's all right.' Tom gave Sarah a severe glance. 'It wouldn't have liked being dropped, you know. And it's silly to be frightened of worms. They can't hurt you.'

Was it worse to have a worm on you or to be rescued by your younger brother? Sarah wasn't sure.

'Well, you're frightened of spiders,' she pointed out. 'And worms are much worse because they're all slimy and they don't have feet.'

'What does that matter?'

'It does, that's all. I don't know why, but it does.'

They looked at each other for a moment. Then Sarah giggled, and so did Tom.

'Imagine a worm with feet,' he said in delight.

He could hardly wait to tell the dragon about it.

How Sarah, who could pick spiders up with her bare fingers, had had to be saved from a worm.

How she'd said she didn't like worms because they had no feet, and how *he'd* said, 'Imagine a ...'

All of a sudden Tom stopped laughing.

'What is it?' asked Sarah, between giggles.

Tom looked at her in horror. How could he have forgotten something like that? That night the dragon was not going to come gaily out from under Tom's bed, ready to laugh about Sarah's silliness.

That night the dragon would be lying in wait behind the currant bushes. At Dragonrise, he'd be heading for Sarah's bedroom window. And for Sarah. The thought of it quite spoiled the joke about worms.

Tom set off for his bedroom without another word, a tight knot of dismay forming in his stomach. Why did everything look so different now from the way it had the night before?

He took the stairs slowly, one by one, his thoughts spinning. It was out of the question for the dragon to be allowed to eat Sarah. He could see that now.

But would the dragon see it?

Would there be rules about whether or not a dragon could eat a gift that wasn't a gift any longer?

He stayed upstairs until suppertime, lying on his bed, sucking his thumb and staring at the ceiling.

At last he arrived at some kind of plan.

He would have to lie in bed until about five minutes before Dragonrise. Then he would creep downstairs secretly, sneak out through the front door – not the back, because that would mean going through the kitchen, where his parents were likely to be – and tiptoe round to the back garden. Then it was just a question of finding the dragon and persuading him that his meal was off. It wasn't going to be easy, and he hated to have to disappoint a friend, but it had to be done.

It was a very jumpy Tom who put his head round the bedroom door that evening to peer down the stairs. He could feel his heart racing as he inched his way along, remembering just in time not to tread on the third stair from the bottom that always squeaked. It would be easy enough to invent an excuse if his father or mother came out of the living room and saw him, but it would complicate his plans frightfully. He *had* to get out to the garden unnoticed somehow or he wouldn't be able to stop the dragon making a meal of Sarah.

At the foot of the stairs Tom took a deep breath. The next thing he knew, he was outside the front door. He pushed it gently almost shut and let his breath out slowly.

'Now, here I go,' he told himself firmly, 'round the corner.'

It was shadowy at the side of the house, and something rustled in the leaves of the privet hedge. Tom couldn't see what it was, and he was glad to reach the back corner of the house, where light was shining out from the gap between the living-room curtains.

Tom crossed his fingers and crawled safely underneath the window. When it was safe, he jumped to his feet and made a dash for the shelter of the currant bushes.

He only hoped he was in time.

'Ouf,' said a familiar voice. 'You're on my tail.'

And there, sure enough, when Tom's eyes had got used to the half-light, was the dragon, ears pricked and eyes a-gleam, like someone whose supper is long overdue.

'How kind of you to come to show me the right window. Not necessary, though. It's that one over there, isn't it?' A tiny tongue of flame flicked out in the direction of Sarah's window.

Yes, that's the right window,' Tom began, 'but –'

'Two minutes to Dragonrise. Two minutes, two minutes,' sang the dragon happily to himself 'Or am I wrong? Is it two minutes or one?' He looked down at his claws, muttering under his breath urgently. 'And seven from ten leaves two, add six makes eleven, multiply by three-eighths is nineteen, take away twelve and adjust for summertime, and there you are, I *was* wrong, it's exactly forty-five seconds to Dragonrise.'

For once Tom was in no mood to put the dragon's arithmetic right. As the dragon surged to his feet, Tom caught hold of his tail in desperation. There was going to be no time for anything but the simple truth.

'Listen, it's all been a mistake. You can't eat Sarah after all.' The tail, which had been quivering under Tom's fingers, went suddenly still.

'Do you mean that I can't eat her tonight?'

Tom didn't answer, staring miserably at the ground beneath the dragon's paws.

The dragon's voice became huskier. 'Or that I can't eat her ever?'

There was no use trying to pretend. 'That you can't eat her ever, I'm afraid.' Tom searched to find the right words, but there weren't any. 'She's my sister, and I was wrong to say you could have her. I'm sorry.'

He sneaked a quick glance to see how the dragon was taking the news. The dragon met his eyes, opened his mouth as if to say something forceful, then shut it again without saying anything. He had discovered that there was something he hated more than missing a meal, and that was seeing a friend unhappy.

'Cheer up, Tom. These things happen.' He drew his claws in carefully to give Tom's shoulder a gentle pat. 'The best of dragons can make a mistake from time to time, and I expect the same happens to people, too. Say no more about it. We'll forget the whole business.'

Tom's eyes filled with tears as his hand went out

to clasp the dragon's paw. He was blinking them away when he became aware of a square of light nearby where none had been before.

The back door had opened.

'Who's out there?' called a voice Tom recognized.

'It's my father,' he whispered, all his relief turning in an instant to dismay. 'What shall I do? I'll get into awful trouble if he finds me out here. I was supposed to be in bed hours ago.'

'Leave it to me,' breathed the dragon into Tom's ear. Before Tom could ask what he was going to do, the dragon was gone.

Tom's father took a step off the back porch into the garden.

It was at this point that something took place about which people were to argue enjoyably for the next three weeks.

Some said it was a meteor bursting into fire over Wetherburn Common.

Some said it was a flying saucer.

The children who were up late enough to be eye-witnesses thought it was the beginning of a fireworks display, and one elderly gentleman stubbornly insisted it was a Russian invasion.

All that was ever settled was that for a full thirty seconds after Mr Smith stepped outside, the sky to the east was lit up with shooting tongues of flame, as dazzling as diamonds and as beautiful as the sun. Mr Smith must have run round to the front of the house to watch, and so must Mrs Smith, because that's where they found themselves when the display ended as abruptly and mysteriously as it had begun.

They looked at each other in silence. Before they had recovered, Mr Beakins from next door called to them.

'Did you see that? I mean, did you *see* that?' His voice croaked with emotion. 'I've never seen anything like it. Never. And look at poor old Rusty. It's given him a proper turn.'

That was certainly true. The shivering dog was trying to bury itself in the shadow under the hedge between the two gardens.

Mrs Smith gave a gasp. 'What about the children?'

But when she ran upstairs to see if they were all right, there was nothing to worry about. Sarah was deep in a mystery story, and quite unaware that anything out of the ordinary had happened. Tom was fast asleep. His mother tiptoed out again, relieved.

As soon as the bedroom door shut, Tom's eyes opened.

'Dragon?' he whispered. 'Dragon, are you there?'

There was no reply.

I can thank him tomorrow night, thought Tom. But it gave him a strange, lonely feeling not to have the dragon down underneath his bed to talk to, and he lay awake for a long time watching the shadows sway across the ceiling before he finally fell asleep.

Chapter Ten

The day after the dragon had almost eaten Sarah could hardly have been worse if the dragon actually *had* eaten her. Tom couldn't keep his mind on anything he was supposed to be doing at school. Mrs Steel was not pleased.

Halfway through the afternoon she called Tom over to her desk. She pointed to one of the problems he had done that morning.

'Tom, what do you get when you take thirteen from seventeen?'

Tom thought hard, in case there was a catch. 'Four?' he suggested cautiously.

'Exactly,' said Mrs Steel. 'If you take thirteen from seventeen, the answer is four. So why have you written forty-one instead?'

'Oh,' said Tom.

There was more. 'Is this –' here Mrs Steel pointed to another sheet of Tom's work '– is this the best you can manage? I thought you were supposed to be drawing a picture of Jane and Peter having fun in their tree house.'

Tom looked at the drawing, and was startled to find that he had drawn a green spiky dragon underneath a tree. He explained that he hadn't had time to put the tree house in. Or Jane and Peter either.

'Then why,' asked Mrs Steel reasonably, 'why waste time drawing in hedgehogs? And if you must draw one, why make it so big and the wrong colour?' She shook her head as she sent him back to his seat. It was disappointing when a promising child like Tom Smith produced work like that. He'd been doing so well lately, too.

If the day was unsatisfactory, the night was worse.

Dragonrise came and went without the dragon.

Tom got so tired of jumping in and out of his bed to look for him that he took his pillow down onto the floor and lay there instead.

There were lots of possible explanations for the dragon not turning up.

The clock might be fast (but it wasn't).

Dragonrise might come later on Tuesdays (but he knew it didn't).

The dragon might be waiting until everything was absolutely quiet (but it had been for half an hour at least).

The dragon had overslept after the unusually energetic flame-throwing of the night before (but he didn't believe that either).

When nine o'clock and then ten o'clock came and still no dragon appeared, Tom admitted what he had really known deep inside all along.

The dragon was never coming back.

He had thrown one flame too many and been sentenced by the Dragonwatch to exile in Wales.

Tom buried his head in the pillow and wept.

Only one thing happened to brighten Tom's life in the days that followed. At breakfast Tom's mother told Sarah and Tom that they were all going to go away when the school's half-term holiday came, in a few weeks' time.

There were two cottages they could rent. One was in Scotland. It was only a few minutes' walk from the sea. It had a stream they could fish in, and a little boat they could take out (only on the stream, and only if they had a grown-up with them, added Mrs Smith). It sounded wonderful.

The other cottage was in Wales. It was on the cliffs above a little harbour, it had a big garden, and –

'Let's go there,' shouted Tom.

His mother was relieved. He'd been looking so miserable for the past few days that she'd been beginning to think he was about to come down with chicken pox.

'The Scotland one sounds nicer.' That was Sarah, of course. But Tom pleaded so hard to go to Wales that he got his way.

One early June morning, the sun shining into Mrs Steel's classroom saw all the children at work writing about what they had done at half term.

'I went to my Grandma's. It were hot in the train. It were a long way. I were sik.'

'I had a kwiet tim. The TV was browkin.'

'I got basht by my bruver. I wint skaytin tweyes. I fell ovur.'

'I looked for dragons in Whales. I did'nt find any. It was'nt the rigth part.'

Sumtymes I wunder why I bover, thought Mrs Steel as she put their work away with a sigh.

It was strange how Tom Smith had got this thing about dragons. There was more to him than met the eye, she thought and gave him special attention for the rest of term. Dragons went on popping up in unexpected places in his work from time to time, but she found herself almost looking forward to them.

Tom did better that term than he ever had before. Sarah was almost jealous.

Towards the end of July, when term was nearly over and Tom was practising running so that he could beat John Murphy on Sports Day, and Sarah was coaching Amanda for the eighty-metres skipping, a postcard came for Tom.

'At least, I *think* that says Tom,' said Mrs Smith, puzzling over the writing, which was shaky, straggly, and an unusual shade of greenish brown.

The card showed a fiery sun sinking behind a range of jagged purple mountains, with 'A Welcome from Wales' written in green across the sky.

The message was short. 'Things not as bad as they might be. Wish you or Gawain were here. Love.' There was no signature. In fact there wasn't even a stamp, and when Mr Smith tried to decipher the postmark, it seemed to contain nothing but a string of l's.

Sarah said that the postcard must have come from John Murphy, who was the only person she knew whose writing was bad enough.

Mr and Mrs Smith thought – but didn't say – that the card was probably for someone else entirely. On the other hand, it was hard to see what the address could be if it wasn't 27 Wellington Gardens.

Tom never said who he thought had sent the card, but he pinned it up in his room beside the drawing of Dragonrise, and kept it for ever more.